To Elwyr

Many Years of
Joy, Happiness + Love

Ed McCaul

Published by CelebrityPress®, Orlando, FL.
CelebrityPress® is a registered trademark.
Printed in the United States of America.

ISBN: 978-1-7322843-6-4
LCCN: 2018956958

This publication is designed to provide accurate and authoritative information with regard to the subject matter covered. It is sold with the understanding that the publisher is not engaged in rendering legal, accounting, or other professional advice. If legal advice or other expert assistance is required, the services of a competent professional should be sought. The opinions expressed by the authors in this book are not endorsed by CelebrityPress® and are the sole responsibility of the author rendering the opinion.

Most CelebrityPress® titles are available at special quantity discounts for bulk purchases for sales promotions, premiums, fundraising, and educational use. Special versions or book excerpts can also be created to fit specific needs.

For more information, please write:
CelebrityPress®
520 N. Orlando Ave, #2
Winter Park, FL 32789
or call 1.877.261.4930

Visit us online at: www.CelebrityPressPublishing.com

Leo Learns About Life

CelebrityPress®
Winter Park, Florida

Contents

Say Hi To Leo!

Leo is a playful puppy who enjoys experiencing the world around him. Leo loves to laugh, play with his toys, and spend time with the people he loves. More importantly, he loves to discover new things! Luckily for Leo, it's a great, big world filled with all kinds of lessons to learn. Even better, he has a bunch of wonderful friends by his side to help him along the way!

Leo's friends teach him some important lessons that he'll use throughout his whole life. Come explore with Leo, and his friends, and discover all the wonderful things Leo learns (and you can too!) in *Leo Learns About Life*.

Leo Follows His Heart

By: Shaunequa Jordan

It was the perfect day to go for a walk around the neighborhood thought Leo. He went outside and started strolling along the sidewalk. He loved being outside in the fresh air.

As Leo continued down the path, he ran into his neighbor, Shaunequa.

"Hey Leo, we both had the same idea! It's such a nice day out I had to be in the sunshine," said Shaunequa.

"Me too!" said Leo. "It's nice to see you, do you want to walk with me?"

"I'd love to," answered Shaunequa.

The two continued around the block together when all of the sudden they heard the happy melody of an ice cream truck!

"Ice cream!!" yelled Leo. "That would make today even better!" he said.

"Come on," said Shaunequa, "let's go get some!"

Leo ran over to the truck with Shaunequa following closely. As he waited in line for his turn to order, he looked at the long list of things he could choose from. There were ice cream sandwiches in three different flavors, fudge bars, orange creamsicles, strawberry shortcake bars, and the popsicles shaped like cartoon characters with bubble gum eyes! Leo started to feel a little overwhelmed, how

was he going to decide?

Shaunequa noticed the shift in her friend and asked him what was the matter.

"I just don't know what to pick," said Leo, "there are so many choices."

Luckily, Shaunequa knew just what to do.

"Close your eyes and picture enjoying some ice cream. Your heart will tell you what you really want," said Shaunequa.

Leo closed his eyes and imagined sitting on a bench with his treat. In his hand was the most scrumptious looking strawberry shortcake bar. He could almost taste the flavor in his mouth already.

Leo opened his eyes back up and exclaimed, "I know what I want!"

"I thought you might," smiled Shaunequa.

The two ordered and went over to the nearby bench to enjoy their desserts.

"You know, Leo, that little trick can work for any decision—big or small. Whether you're trying to pick a food or you're trying to decide what sport to tryout for. If you look to your heart it will always tell you the right decision for you!"

"Really?" asked Leo. "My heart hasn't ever talked to me before."

"Are you sure?" questioned Shaunequa. "Have you ever had happy butterflies in your tummy when you were excited to do something? That's your heart making sure you know you're making a good choice. Or, maybe you did something without thinking and suddenly your stomach felt like it was tied in knots.

That's how you know your heart doesn't agree with your decision."

"Cool," exclaimed Leo as he finished off his strawberry shortcake bar. "It worked really well for picking out my ice cream. That was delicious!"

Shaunequa laughed, "I'm glad you enjoyed it. I bet you'll find that it'll work well for a lot of things. If you always listen to your heart Leo, you'll never go wrong."

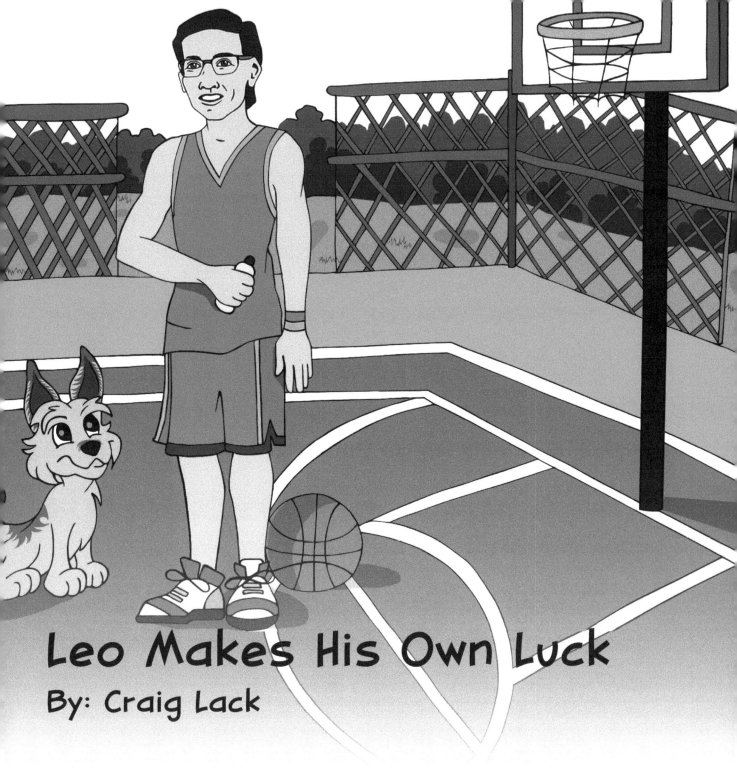

Leo Makes His Own Luck

By: Craig Lack

Leo was walking past the basketball court when he saw his friend, Craig, shooting hoops by himself. He was really good! He could dribble the ball in all different directions, and had even made some trick shots. Leo decided to stay and watch.

As Craig stopped to get some water, he noticed Leo looking at him. He called over, "Hey Leo, would you like to play?"

"No, thank you," said Leo, "I can't play like you, you're so lucky to be good at basketball."

"Come on over and have a seat," called Craig. Leo walked over and sat on the bench.

"I want to talk about why you said I'm lucky to be good at basketball," said Craig.

"Well," said Leo, "some people are really lucky to be good at sports, I can play but I'm not as good as you."

"Luck doesn't have anything to do with it," said Craig. "I've worked really hard to be good. I practiced a lot, I had coaches and mentors to help me and give me advice. I've even read books about basketball, and my favorite players, so I could learn more."

"Wow!" replied Leo. "You did all that just to be better

at basketball?"

"I do that for everything I care about. I'm the one who decides how my life is going to go, so I make sure to create my own luck by taking action. If you want to be good at a certain sport, or a subject in school, then you have to make that happen by getting help, always practicing and trying your best. It works the same when you get older too, for your career! Successful people make their own luck."

"It works for anything?" questioned Leo. "What if I wanted to be an astronaut, a Chef, or a Detective?"

Craig chuckled, "Life has no limits, Leo. You can be any of those things! Read books on astronauts. Have your mom teach you a recipe. Talk to a policeman at career day at school. Once you decide what you want, keep focusing on your goal and always take advantage of the opportunity to learn."

"I can do that!" exclaimed Leo.

"I know you can. Why don't we start with basketball?" said Craig. "With a little practice we'll have you making baskets in no time."

"That sounds fun," said Leo.

Leo picked up the ball and ran onto the court. He started practicing his dribbling and Craig gave him some tips so his paw would have more control over the ball. Then they played a game in order to help Leo work on his free throws. By the end of the afternoon Leo had made a few shots and he was very proud of

himself.

"Good effort today Leo, I'm so glad you decided to play after all," said Craig.

"Me too!" said Leo. "Pretty soon my friends at school will think I'm the lucky one at basketball, but we know better, don't we?"

"We sure do!" said Craig laughing.

Leo Accepts Change
By: Brittany Barocsi

Leo was so upset. His kayaking trip for this weekend got canceled. He planned on having so much fun, but now he couldn't go. Leo decided to call his friend Brittany. She always made him feel better.

"Hello," said Brittany as she answered the phone.

"Hi Brittany," said Leo. "I'm really sad, my kayaking trip got canceled this weekend."

"I'm sorry your plans changed, Leo."

"I hate when things change," replied Leo.

"Can you come over to my house on Saturday night? Maybe I can cheer you up," said Brittany.

"I don't know if it will work, but I'll come over," agreed Leo.

On Saturday evening, Leo headed over to Brittany's house. He'd been blue all day wishing he was kayaking on the river. However, when he walked through the backyard gate, he was happily surprised to see a tent and a fire!

"Hi," called Leo. "What is this?"

"Hey Leo, I figured a campout was just what you needed. We've got treats to cook over the fire, ghost stories, and board games!"

The two played games until Leo's tummy started rumbling. Then they put some popcorn on the fire and searched the yard for the perfect marshmallow

sticks. As Leo and Brittany sat by the fire, roasting their marshmallows for s'mores, they both had big smiles.

"This turned into a really good night," said Leo.

"I'm glad," said Brittany. "Leo, things throughout life are always going to change. Sometimes those changes are small, like having your trip canceled. Other times those changes are going to be big, like maybe moving to a new house or starting a new school."

"I'm moving?!" cried Leo.

"No Silly, you aren't moving. Someday you might though, like when you go to college or start a new job. Those are huge changes. They're exciting too, but that doesn't mean that they won't be a little scary at the same time."

"How can I make changes easier?" asked Leo.

"Sometimes you just have to accept that things need to change. Life can't stay the same forever. Otherwise, we would be bored! You just need to be brave and know that changes happen for a reason, even if we don't understand the reason at the time. That way whether the change is big or small, exciting or scary, you'll be confident that you can handle it."

"Do I have to handle them all by myself?" asked Leo.

"Absolutely not, you can always call your friends and family! I bet some of them will feel the same way sometimes. Plus, talking to someone who understands makes you feel better. It's nice knowing you're not alone. Or, just spending time with friends to get your mind off your worries helps."

"Like tonight," yelled Leo.

"Exactly! I'll always be here to help—for changes big and small!" replied Brittany.

Then the friends assembled their s'mores and settled in for some of their favorite ghost stories.

"Some changes aren't so bad after all," thought Leo.

Leo Contributes To His Community

By: Perminder Chohan

Leo had toys everywhere! He was laying in the living room surrounded by all his favorites, but he still had a bunch in their cubbies in his playroom upstairs too. He was racing his fire truck around and saving all his townspeople from imaginary fires when the doorbell rang.

Leo got up and opened the door to see Perminder there.

"Hello!" Leo greeted his friend. "Come on in."

"Hey there, Leo!" said Perminder as he walked inside. "Oh wow! Look at all these toys. That's actually what I wanted to talk to you about."

"You wanted to talk about my toys?" asked Leo.

"Yes! Our community is hosting a toy drive and I wanted to know if you'd like to help," said Perminder.

"A toy drive," said Leo, "that sounds fun. Sure, I'll bring toys with me and we can drive them around."

Perminder laughed, "That's not exactly how it works, Leo. A toy drive is when people in the community donate their toys and we give them to other kids who need them."

"Oh!" said Leo. "No thanks. I need my toys."

"You don't have to donate if you don't want to, but I was hoping you'd like to give some and contribute

to your community, since they do so much for you," replied Perminder. Leo had that sinking feeling in his tummy that he'd done something wrong.

"What's contributing?" asked Leo.

"Contributing is giving," said Perminder. "If you think of it, the community does all kinds of things for you. For example, I know you love coming to the movies in the park to watch your favorite movies on the big screen. Also, the community hosted the 4th of July BBQ and you got to eat hot dogs and play on the giant bounce house and watch fireworks."

"So, giving to the toy drive is a way for you to say 'thank you' for all the good things the community does for you. It shows you like living in a place where people want to help one another and do fun things together," explained Perminder.

"I do like all of those things," replied Leo, "but do I really have to give up all my toys?"

"Of course not!" said Perminder. "You don't have to give them all away, but maybe there are some you don't play with anymore that another little boy or girl, who doesn't have as much as you, would love to play with."

"Oh!" exclaimed Leo, "I want to contribute now! I have some toys upstairs I don't really play with anymore. Do you think some other kids would like those?"

"I think there are kids who would love those toys, Leo. Thank you for being willing to give back to your community!" said Perminder.

"I want to show that I like living here too. Is there anything else I can do?" asked Leo.

"Well, I do need someone to volunteer to help hand out the toys to the kids and see how happy it makes them. Do you think you could do that?" asked Perminder.

"I sure can!" replied Leo, smiling.

Leo Discovers the Power of Words

By: Nina M. Kelly

Leo walked out the front door and over to the house next door. Nina was on her front porch again watching the people walk by on the way to the park. She did that often and Leo liked to go sit and talk with her.

"Hi Nina," Leo said as he sat next to her on the steps. "That girl who walked by looked really sad," he commented.

"Hey Leo! Yes, she did. I think someone must have hurt her feelings," answered Nina.

"That's silly," said Leo, "I don't let people hurt my feelings."

"I bet that's not true," said Nina. "Words are very powerful and they affect us more than we realize. If I told you, 'Leo, you're a great Frisbee player and I'm proud of how hard you practice,' how does that make you feel?"

Leo smiled, "That makes me happy, and I want to keep trying hard."

"Exactly," said Nina. "Here is another example, I've only seen you wear your red backpack to school lately, why haven't you used your blue one? It was your favorite."

"Charlie made fun of it, and I didn't want to wear it anymore," said Leo.

"That's what I mean," said Nina, "Charlie's words influenced you. The things that people say matter.

Sometimes they make us feel happy, loved or confident. And other times they make us frustrated, angry or sad. We should always try to be kind and encourage people. Your words could help make their whole day better."

"I never thought about that before," said Leo.

"My Mom taught me to 'guard my tongue' when I was a little girl, and to think before I speak. She even sang a song about it," said Nina.

"Can I hear it?" asked Leo.

"Words can heal
Words can harm
Words can make us happy
And even forlorn

Words can bring joy
For each girl and boy
Words can also carry sadness and woe
How easily we let them flow...

Words can be spoken, written, or sung.
Words have great power and once released can rarely
be undone," sang Nina.

"That was wonderful!" exclaimed Leo. "Can you write
it down for me? It's my turn to do a puppet show at
school and my friends would like it too!"

"Absolutely," exclaimed Nina. "I'll even help you
practice!"

"I'm so excited," yelled Leo. "I'm going to get my
puppets right now!"

Leo ran all the way home and grabbed his puppets
and made it back to Nina's house in just a few minutes.

She had covered a table with a sheet in her backyard for Leo to sit behind and was just finishing writing the song down for him. Nina helped Leo set up his puppets and then sat on the ground to enjoy the show.

He acted out his little skit and sang her song joyfully. She was very proud of him for wanting to teach his classmates about the power of their words too, and couldn't wait to hear all about it!

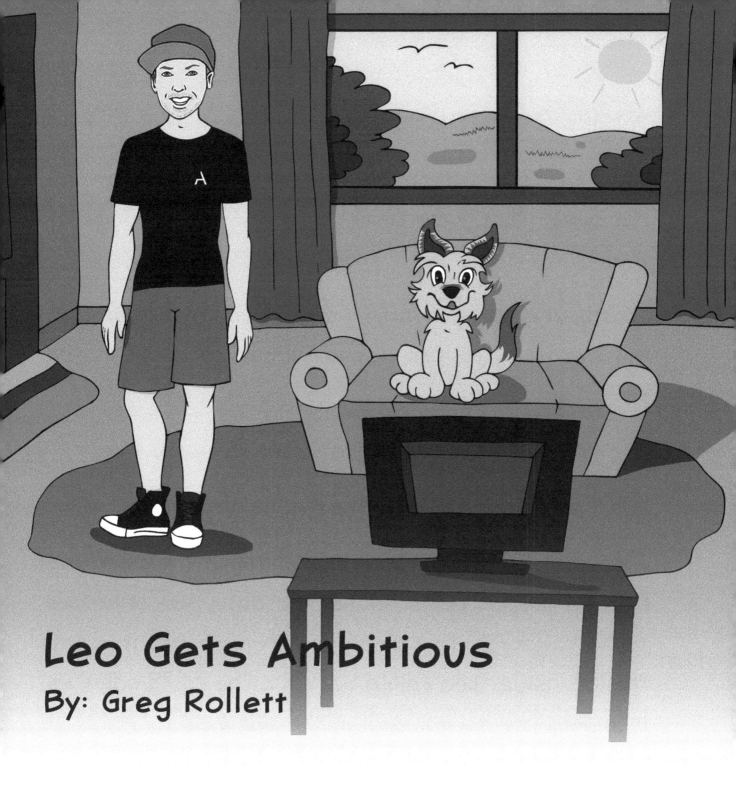

Leo Gets Ambitious
By: Greg Rollett

The sun was shining and it was a beautiful day outside when Leo's friend, Greg, knocked on the door. Leo called, "Come in," but he didn't get up from the couch. He was too focused on what was on TV.

"What's up, Leo?" said Greg.

"Hi Greg. I'm watching the Doggie Olympics. They can run super fast, jump really high and do all kinds of tricks."

"That's awesome, buddy. I'm glad you're enjoying it, but I came by to see if you wanted to come to the park," said Greg.

"No thanks," said Leo. "I just want to watch this."

"Ok," said Greg. "I'll stop here again on my way back."

A couple hours later Greg was done at the park and headed toward Leo's house. The door was unlocked so he knocked a few times and then opened it to yell "Hello" inside. Leo called back that he could come in, it looked like he was still in the same spot.

"Are you still on the couch, didn't you do anything today?" Greg asked.

"I wanted to see this. These dogs are all so cool. They can do all these amazing things. I wish I could

be like them," said Leo.

"You can do cool things too, Leo, if you get off the couch and find some ambition," said Greg.

"What's ambition?" Leo asked.

"Ambition is when you really want to do something, so you come up with a plan to make it happen. You set goals for yourself and you feel really good when you reach them," explained Greg. "I have an idea! If you want to be like the dogs in the Olympics, let's sign up for a 5K. It's a race we can run together. I can come over and help you practice so you're ready for race day."

"That sounds awesome," said Leo. "Do you really think I can do it?"

"I think you can do anything you want! It might take some hard work, but as long as you're ambitious and you really want to achieve your goal you can make it happen. I'll be here to help and encourage you too!" Greg exclaimed.

For a few weeks, Greg and Leo practiced running and jumping and even doing monkey bars, just in case. Finally, it was race day and Leo was so excited! The two ran through the whole course and there were even people cheering for them. At the end of the race Leo and Greg both got medals!

"This was so fun," Leo said. "Look I even have my own medal now, just like the dogs in the Olympics!"

"I'm so proud of you, Leo! You worked really hard. But, just because this race is done doesn't mean you give up on being ambitious! Now that you know you can do it, you can set even bigger goals."

"Don't worry, I've got another idea already!" said Leo winking.

Leo Finds His Self-Confidence

By: Gerri Asbury

Leo was very small compared to other pups his age. He loved investigating everything outside, examining bugs, and observing birds. But Leo often felt lonely and worried that his classmates thought he was too Little and Extremely Odd. That is why Leo always looked forward to "Super Saturdays." Those were his PAW Power Adventure days with Ms. Asbury, a Master Wordsmith. Leo loved the way she turned words into messages that made him feel special by focusing on his own PAW (Phenomenal Abilities Within) Power. Today they were going to the beach!

"Hello!" called Leo as he ran towards her through the sand.

Ms. Asbury replied, "How's my Little Expert Observer today?"

Before he could respond, Leo noticed that the white caps were rolling in and the kids' kickboards were being swept off the shore. Leo quickly dove into the water to retrieve the kickboards. One by one he brought all eight back to shore. The kids were so excited to see Leo in action; they jumped up and down to cheer him on.

Leo was surprised to see the letters "L" "E" "O" on the first three boards. Then he heard the kids' chanting,

"Leo is...Lovable, Extraordinary, and Observant!"

The next board Leo retrieved contained a giant heart with a paw print in the center of it, followed by boards with the letters "H" " E" "R" and "O."

Leo felt a deep sense of pride as he sat next to the kickboards on the beach. Ms. Asbury took an instant photograph as the kids gathered around Leo petting and thanking him for being their HERO (Helping Everyone Reassuring Ourselves).

Ms. Asbury spoke softly as she smiled and complimented him, "Leo, you demonstrated great self-confidence this morning. You are a shining STAR (Sharing Talents Abilities Resources)."

At lunchtime, Ms. Asbury shared a flyer about a program starting that afternoon at the library. As Leo read the words aloud, "Needed: Dedicated Obedient Guardians for Service," his eyes opened wide!

"That spells DOGS!!" exclaimed Leo.

"You're right, Leo, and I have a special gift for you to wear if you'd like to go," said Ms. Asbury. Leo was so excited, he opened the box and found a green harness with "Service Dog in Training" written on it.

"At last, my own real super hero uniform!!" yelled Leo joyfully.

Leo's tail wagged nonstop all the way to the library. Upon entering, the Librarian welcomed them and asked Leo, "Are you very observant?"

Leo responded without hesitating, "Yes, I am Loyal

and <u>E</u>xtremely <u>O</u>bservant (LEO), that's me!"

Leo was ready and eager to train to become a therapeutic safety service dog. He kept his photo from the beach in his pocket so he'd always remember the day he rediscovered his special talents and found his self-confidence. He was becoming the HERO he was born to be!!

Ms. Asbury's eyes twinkled as she began planning the next PAW Power Adventure day with Leo.

Leo Understands Integrity

By: Edward Mafoud

Today was going to be a good day! Leo was going to visit Ed, one of his good friends and the President of Damascus Bakery. He always had lots of tasty treats.

Leo knocked on the back door of the house and Ed welcomed him into the kitchen. Ed's bakery made lots of specialty breads, but today the whole room smelled like peanut butter cookies, Leo's favorite!

"Hi Ed, it smells so good in here," exclaimed Leo.

"Hey there, buddy," replied Ed, "I did some baking today."

Just when Leo was about to ask for a cookie, Ed's phone started ringing.

"Hold on Leo, let me grab that and I'll be right back," said Ed.

As Leo looked around, he spotted the cookies cooling on the counter. Ed wouldn't mind if he tasted one, right? He wouldn't even know! Leo crept over and snuck a cookie. It was the best cookie he ever had. So he took another one, and another. Before he knew it, he had eaten a whole row of cookies! Leo heard Ed walking in the hallway and scurried back to his seat.

"Sorry Leo! So, would you like to try a cookie?" asked

Ed as he looked over at the counter.

"Wait a minute, I had six rows of cookies. Do you know what happened to them?" questioned Ed as he spotted the cookie crumbs on Leo's fur.

"I don't know where they went," said Leo shrugging.

"Well then, I think it's time we had a talk about integrity," said Ed.

"What's integrity?" asked Leo.

"Integrity is when you do the right thing, even when no one is around to see your actions" replied Ed. "People who show integrity know the difference between right and wrong. They understand how important it is to be honest and make good decisions. No one wants to be around people they can't trust."

Leo thought about what Ed was saying. He felt really bad about what he'd done. He wanted to be trustworthy and show integrity too!

"Ed, I ate the cookies. I'm sorry; I should have asked if I could have one. I shouldn't have lied either. Does that mean I don't have integrity?" asked Leo.

"No," smiled Ed, "You did the right thing by admitting it and apologizing. That means you know you were wrong, but next time you need to make a better choice. I know it was tempting to see your favorite cookies sitting on the counter, but there will be lots of situations when doing the right thing is hard, and people need to know they can count on you to make good choices anyway."

"I promise to do better," said Leo. "Is there anything I can do to make it right?"

"I have some extra dough, why don't you help me make replacement cookies," answered Ed.

"I'd love to," said Leo.

They both wore big smiles as Ed taught Leo how to roll the dough and cut it into the perfect cookie shape!

Leo Learns To Help

By: Sheri Hays

Leo rushed all the way to the library. It was Wednesday and Ms. Sheri was going to be there for story time! Each week she read to all the kids and pups. Leo always looked forward to it.

"Hello everyone," said Ms. Sheri as they sat cross-legged on the floor. "Today's story is called *Reese's Rescue*. Let's get started!"

Once upon a time there was a puppy named Reese who lived with his best friend, a boy named Ben.

Ms. Sheri showed the children the picture inside the book.

"Hey, that looks like me!" called Leo.

"It sure does, Leo! Let's see what happens." She continued reading...

One day Reese and Ben were playing outside when Ben threw the ball into the woods. Reese ran in to look for it, but he couldn't find it anywhere. He went deeper and deeper in until he was very lost. He didn't know how to get home!

The sun began to set and Reese began to shiver. His tummy started growling too, he was so hungry! And he kept hearing all these noises; he got more scared with every sound. Reese began to cry, not sure if he would ever find his way home.

Just as Reese began to give up hope, he saw a light shining through the trees. There was a house on the edge of the woods. A lady inside came out and called to him, but Reese was too afraid to go over. Luckily, the woman was very kind. She put some food and water in bowls and brought them outside for him. She also put a warm blanket into a cardboard box next to the food. As soon as she went back inside, Reese ran over to the food and ate every bite! Then he curled up into the blanket, finally feeling warm and safe.

The next morning, Reese woke up to a sunny day. Filled with hope, he ran along the road until he saw Ben calling his name. Reese ran up to him and hugged him so tight!

A little later when the woman looked outside her window, Reese had already gone. She would never know what happened to him. However, her willingness to help had rescued Reese and made him and Ben so happy!

"Who can tell me the moral of the story?" asked Ms. Sheri. Leo raised his paw and she pointed at him to speak.

"I think it is that you should always try to help people," said Leo.

"Very good," said Ms. Sheri. "The woman's kindness saved Reese and brought both him and Ben so much happiness. She helped Reese without expecting anything in return. We should always do our best to help people, you never know how much joy you might bring!"

After they finished their discussion, everyone clapped and hugged Ms. Sheri goodbye.

"Thanks for sharing Reese's story, Ms. Sheri," said Leo. "I'm going to always help people whenever I can."

"I'm glad you were here, Leo. I know you will!" exclaimed Ms. Sheri.

Leo's Thoughts Are Powerful

By: Rosie Unite

Leo heard a knock and ran to let his friend Rosie inside. She was going to watch the new baby while his parents were out.

"Hi Leo," said Rosie as she hugged him. "Where's your

baby sister? I can't wait to meet Brooke!"

"Hello, Rosie. She's over there," Leo said. "Everyone is so excited about her." He didn't look very excited though.

"It's fun to have a new family member," said Rosie, as she cuddled Brooke.

"If you say so," sighed Leo. So far, he wasn't happy about it. All she did was cry and hog all the attention. Nobody wanted to play with him all week. Leo was jealous.

"Is everything OK, Leo?" Rosie asked, seeing him unhappy.

"My tummy hurts," said Leo. "I'm going to lie down on the sofa."

"I hope you feel better," said Rosie. "Brooke and I will join you, and we can watch a movie together." Rosie then put Brooke in Leo's favorite spot. He couldn't believe it. That was his special place on the sofa! His stomach hurt even more.

As Rosie picked a movie, Brooke started to cry. Leo was so tired of her crying that he decided to try

something new. He licked her whole face. To Leo's surprise, Brooke stopped crying!

Excited, he wondered what else he could do to make Brooke like him, so she wouldn't cry so much. He smiled at her and nuzzled her neck very softly. She giggled and wrapped her tiny fingers around his paw.

Leo's heart swelled. He was so happy he could make his little sister laugh, and she wanted to be near him too!

Rosie saw Leo's giant grin. "Feeling better?" she asked.

"Yes, and my tummy ache is gone!" squealed Leo.

"Were you jealous of Brooke? You weren't excited for me to meet her, were you?" asked Rosie.

"Maybe a little," replied Leo.

"That's why you didn't feel good. Our thoughts are very powerful! When we think negatively and feel emotions like jealousy, anger, and fear we hurt our bodies. The opposite is true, too. When we think positively and feel emotions like thankfulness, love, and compassion our bodies are healthier. When you made Brooke laugh you felt great, didn't you?" questioned Rosie.

"Yeah!" exclaimed Leo, "Can our thoughts really do that?"

"Absolutely! That's why it's important to be optimistic, confident, and kind to yourself and others! When you think mean or sad thoughts it makes you feel bad. Sometimes your stomach or head will hurt, or maybe you won't sleep well. When you are happy and helping others you feel strong and energized. Your thoughts

are so powerful that they can change your body and make you feel like you can do anything! You become your own superhero! Actually, I'm going to call you Loveable Leo!" squealed Rosie.

"Wow! I'm a superhero! I guess I have to keep being nice to Brooke then, right?" asked Leo.

Rosie laughed, "It sure does! I know you'll be a wonderful big brother. Brooke is lucky to have you."

Leo's heart felt even bigger!

Leo Practices Gratitude

By: Lindsay Dicks

Tuesday was one of Leo's favorite days, because every week he went over to Lindsay's house and they did arts and crafts together! He never knew what kind of project they'd get to do, but they were always fun.

Leo checked his backpack to make sure he had everything he might need: colored paper, crayons, markers, stickers, scissors and a glue stick. Check! It looked like he was all ready to go, so he took his bag and headed down the street. When he got to Lindsay's house she was outside by the mailbox.

"Hi Leo," Lindsay said, as she placed her envelopes inside the box.

"Hi Lindsay, what are you mailing?" questioned Leo.

"I have some thank you notes I'm sending to some of my friends and family," answered Lindsay. "I'm practicing gratitude."

"I say thank you to people," said Leo. "But what does gratitude mean?"

"Come on in the house and I'll explain," said Lindsay with a smile.

They walked inside and Leo sat down at the kitchen table where they always did their best projects. Lindsay

sat next to Leo and helped him take his supplies out of his backpack.

"Well, Leo, gratitude is when you're thankful and appreciate the different things people do for you. It's more than just saying thank you to be polite. Being polite is also important, but gratitude is going a step further and feeling grateful for that act of kindness someone has shown you."

"I don't think I understand," said Leo. "When I say thank you, I mean it."

"I know you do," said Lindsay. "And that's great, you should say thank you! But sometimes it means a lot to people when you express how much something means to you beyond just saying thank you. It lets them know that their act of kindness or their friendship is important to you. Does that make sense?"

"I get it now," said Leo. "I have an idea! For our arts and crafts today would you help me write my own thank you cards so I can practice gratitude too?"

"Of course, Leo, I think that's a great idea," smiled Lindsay.

The two of them worked on writing a few notes to different people that were important to Leo and they added stickers and drew pictures to make them extra special. Once they were done they walked out to Lindsay's mailbox together so he could put his notes in the mail too.

Leo put his cards inside and closed the mailbox, but he still had one envelope in his paw.

"This one is for you," said Leo as he handed the card to Lindsay. "Thank you for always doing fun things with me and teaching me about gratitude today. I love spending time with you."

"You're so welcome, and I love spending time with you too," said Lindsay and she gave Leo a big hug.

Leo Protects His Smile

By: Dr. Darren Tong

Leo's favorite show ended and he turned off the TV. He threw out his candy wrappers, put on his pajamas, and went to sleep.

The next morning, Leo woke up with terrible tooth pain! Leo was worried about visiting the dentist, but his tooth really hurt, so he'd have to go.

A little later, Leo sat in the Dentist's waiting room. He was very nervous. The door opened, and a Doctor walked out with a friendly smile.

"Hi Leo, I'm Dr. Darren, I heard you have a toothache and need my help! I'm here to take good care of you, please come with me."

He brought Leo to an area where a machine took pictures of his teeth. Then Leo followed him into another room and sat in a big, soft chair.

"How are you feeling?" asked Dr. Darren, as an assistant gave Leo some cool glasses to wear during the appointment.

"My tooth hurts," said Leo, "and I'm a little scared."

Dr. Darren smiled, "Leo, we're here to help you. We'll make sure your mouth is feeling much better after your visit! Why don't we start by cleaning your teeth, and I'll look at your x-rays."

After a few minutes passed, Dr. Darren announced,

"Well, Leo, the 'sugar bugs' have made a hole, or cavity, in your tooth. Are you finding it hard to keep your teeth clean?"

"Yes," said Leo, looking embarrassed. "Dr. Darren, I really like candies and sometimes I'm too tired to brush my teeth before bed."

Dr. Darren spoke in a soft tone, "Leo, you only get one set of adult teeth. You need to take better care of them to keep that nice smile of yours!"

"I love my smile, and I don't want sugar bugs to cause any more toothaches!" said Leo.

"Great!" said Dr. Darren, "I'll clean out those sugar bugs and put a nice 'white filling' in to help your tooth feel better and look shiny again. You're going to promise to eat less candy and brush your teeth after meals, even when you're tired. In six months, after another cleaning, I'm sure you'll be cavity-free!"

Leo was very happy and glad everything was going to be much better now.

Dr. Darren cleaned out the sugar bugs and filled Leo's cavity. Leo was surprised it didn't hurt at all! Dr. Darren was so gentle; he couldn't remember why he was scared of the dentist! Plus, his tooth felt much better. When Leo looked in the mirror his teeth were all white and shiny, he loved how clean they felt.

"For being such a great helper today, you get a goodie bag with a new toothbrush, toothpaste and you can pick a prize from our toy chest. You also get a nice, blue balloon, since it's your favorite color!" said Dr. Darren.

Leo went home smiling and feeling very proud. He was so happy that going to the dentist was very easy, and he was glad that he went today!

Leo Learns How To Fulfill His Musical Dreams

By: Dean Collins

As Leo strolled through town, he liked seeing all the people and hearing the different sounds. Today there was an even better sound than usual. Leo could hear a guitar! As Leo walked across the street he saw a man strumming a guitar and playing a harmonica.

"Wow!" Leo said as he walked over. "You're really good at that. I love the way the guitar and harmonica sounds."

"Well hello there, thank you!" said the man, "I'm Dean, what's your name?"

"I'm Leo!"

"It's nice to meet you, Leo, do you know how to play any instruments?" asked Dean.

"No," replied Leo. "I love the way music sounds, and how happy it makes people. My dream is to play someday. It looks really hard though."

"It's not hard," said Dean. "Sometimes all it takes is one step to set a dream into motion. I'll even help you start. You can come to my music class this afternoon!"

"That sounds great," said Leo, "I'll see you then!"

A few hours later, Leo walked into to the music studio Dean had told him about. Dean introduced him to two

girls he recognized from his neighborhood, Haidyn and Kennedy. Then he handed Leo and Haidyn a guitar while Kennedy was going to learn the harmonica.

Leo kept strumming the strings, but the sound his guitar was making didn't sound anything like Dean's music. "I'm terrible and I don't know how to do this," said Leo.

"Don't worry about how. It's only your first lesson, Leo. Let's work on being positive! Do you want to play a game?" questioned Dean.

"Sure," said Leo.

"O.K., close your eyes and pretend you're a doggy rock star," said Dean. "Picture your dreams and goals fulfilled and feel that happiness."

With a big smile and wagging tail, Leo made believe and imagined himself on stage.

"Now, open your eyes, Leo. Play that game every day with yourself and believe it!" said Dean. "Focus on what you want and the good feeling you get as you take the action needed to get there."

"Wow, that feels great!" said Leo. "I think I found my purpose!"

"Awesome, Leo!" said Dean. "Purpose, passion, goals and vision are all part of my magical music lessons."

"Now let's practice," said Dean. Then he helped Leo put his paws in the right places.

By the end of the lesson, Leo, Haidyn and Kennedy had all learned how to play the song, "If You're Happy

and You Know It, Clap Your Hands." Dean played both instruments at the same time with his invention called Happy Holdo.

"Great job today, everyone! Remember to dream, have fun and practice. I can't wait to teach you to play both instruments at the same time."

"Can I come back for another lesson next week?" asked Leo.

"Of course you can," said Dean.

Leo Treats Others How He'd Like To Be Treated
By: JW Dicks

It was a beautiful spring day outside, and today was going to be extra special. Leo's friend Jack had promised he'd come over to play Frisbee! Leo loved Frisbee!

Once Jack arrived, the two friends walked into the backyard and started to play. Jack tossed the Frisbee high into the air and it soared across the backyard. Leo ran underneath it, making sure he was going to make the catch. Then, with one big jump, he'd catch the Frisbee and run back to Jack.

The two of them played together for a while when suddenly Jack stopped. He was looking toward the edge of the yard. Another gray dog was sitting there watching them.

Jack yelled, "Hello there, what's your name? Would you like to join us?"

"Hi, I'm Sophie. I didn't mean to interrupt. I was just watching, but I don't know how to play," said Sophie.

"That's alright," said Jack, "We can teach you!"

Jack threw the Frisbee into the air and said, "All you have to do is watch the Frisbee and go wherever you think it might land, then try to catch it."

Leo ran over and caught the Frisbee.

"That's good," said Jack, "But let Sophie try to catch a few."

Jack threw the Frisbee again, and Sophie jumped up, but she missed. Jack threw the Frisbee to her two more times, she hadn't caught one yet, but she looked like she was having fun. On the last throw Leo ran over, jumped up, and caught the Frisbee instead. Sophie backed up and let Leo catch all the throws, but she wasn't smiling anymore.

"Why don't we take a break," said Jack. "Leo, can you come here a minute? Sophie, we'll be right back."

Leo and Jack walked inside, but Jack didn't look very happy.

"What's wrong, Jack?"

"Well, I wanted to talk to you about Sophie. I don't think you're treating her very nice, " said Jack.

"I'm not being mean," said Leo, "It's not my fault she's not any good."

"Just because someone isn't as good as you, doesn't mean they shouldn't get to try. You wouldn't like it if someone didn't give you a chance to try, would you?"

"No," said Leo.

"That's what I thought," said Jack. "I know you weren't trying to be mean, but remember to always treat everyone how you'd like to be treated. If you wouldn't like how it feels, then you know you shouldn't ever treat someone else that way. You'd want others to let you play, so you should let Sophie play too."

"Okay," said Leo. "I'll take turns."

As the two walked outside, Leo ran up to Sophie. "Hi Sophie, I'm sorry I kept catching the Frisbee and didn't let you try. If you still want to play with us, we can take turns!"

"I'd like that very much," said Sophie.

Jack, Leo and Sophie started to play with the Frisbee once more and this time everyone had fun. Leo even made a new friend!

Leo's Heart Matters Most
By: Dr. Carmella Montez Knoernschild

The sun was setting and Leo had spent a wonderful day at the fair. The funnel cake, the Ferris wheel, and bumper cars were his favorites so far! Now, he was on his way to the giant swings that lift you up and spin you around when he walked past the fun house mirrors.

Leo looked into the first mirror and smiled. It made him look really short and fat, with his brown fur he looked like a little meatball. The next mirror made him look tall and skinny; he stretched out his neck and pretended to be a giraffe. He giggled at himself. When Leo got to the third mirror it was his normal reflection; he didn't laugh this time. Instead, he looked sad as he stared at himself. Was one ear bigger than the other? Was his fur fluffy enough? Maybe one eye was a little too small?

Leo was so distracted by the mirrors that he didn't notice his friend, Dr. K, watching him.

"What's the matter, Leo?" she asked as she walked toward him.

"Oh, hi Dr. K, what are you doing here?" replied Leo.

"I was enjoying the fair with my family until I saw you looking so sad. Aren't you having fun?" questioned Dr. K.

"I was," said Leo, "until I saw these mirrors. The first two made me look really funny, but this one is normal and I still don't look right."

"First," said Dr. K, "I think you look lovely just the way you are."

"I'm not so sure. In fact, I know you've helped my friend's teeth so they look better, but I'm afraid to show my teeth," said Leo.

"That's true. I help many people have straighter, whiter teeth so they can better enjoy their food and have more confidence. It's okay to feel good about how you look, and to try to look your best. However, you need to understand, it's truly more important to focus on the inside," answered Dr. K.

"What?" asked Leo, "how do I see what I look like on the inside?"

"You can't see it, but you can show it. Have you ever met someone who looked beautiful, but they always treated you mean? Suddenly, they don't look as pretty. Or sometimes you don't think someone is very attractive, but when they are kind and caring you look at them in a new way, right?

"I think I understand," said Leo.

"There is one thing you should always remember, Leo. Your value as a person is not determined by your physical appearance. What makes you beautiful is your big heart. When you are kind to others, that makes you someone I want to be friends with forever!"

Leo felt warm and fuzzy inside. "Thanks, Dr. K. I understand how my inside affects my outside now. I feel better."

"I'm glad I could help! Now, let's do something fun. Do you want to come ride the swings with my family?" asked Dr. K.

"I sure do!" exclaimed Leo.

Leo Finds A Perspective

By: Nick Nanton

Leo was sitting on his porch. The sky was gray and cloudy, and it was raining out. It was going to be a terrible day.

Suddenly, Leo's friend Nick walked up. He shook off his umbrella and they walked inside.

"Hi Leo! How are you?" he said smiling.

"I'm bored," said Leo, "I'm not going to have any fun because it's raining."

"It sounds to me like you need a different perspective," said Nick as he walked down the hall.

Leo started thinking, "What is a perspective? Is it something I can play with?"

A few minutes later, Leo heard Nick laughing in the living room. He took one more look out the window, but it was still rainy out. Maybe he should try this perspective toy too!

Leo walked in the room and there were pillows and blankets everywhere. Even some of the chairs from the kitchen were inside. "Is this what a perspective does?" he asked.

"No, Silly, " said Nick laughing. "A perspective is how you think about something. It's not a game, but if you

focus on happy things, you're sure to have fun!"

Then Leo spotted a bag of his favorite cookies sitting on the other side of the room. Leo took one step toward the cookies before Nick called out, "The floor is hot lava! You can't touch it. You start on that pillow and I'll start on this one. Whoever gets to the cookies first gets to eat them. Ready. Set. Go!"

They both took off jumping from pillow to pillow.

Leo hopped onto a kitchen chair then leaped onto a nearby couch cushion. He almost lost his balance and started laughing as he rolled onto the cushion. "This is so fun!" he yelled.

Nick was halfway across the room when his foot slipped off the edge of a blanket. "Oh no! Now I have to hop on one leg!" He jumped across the blanket onto a nearby pillow and grabbed onto the coffee table so he wouldn't topple over. Leo laughed so hard at his friend bouncing around on only one foot. Then, Leo took one more big jump and he reached the cookies! He'd won! He picked up the bag and walked over to meet Nick who'd sat down in a chair.

"This was the best afternoon EVER!" said Leo. "I didn't know you could have so much fun when it's rainy!"

"That's because you were thinking about things all wrong," said Nick. "You assumed it was going to be a bad day, but just because something isn't going the way you want doesn't mean it's bad. If you try to find the good in every situation, good things will happen!"

"Thanks for teaching me about perspectives! I'm going to do my best to always look for good things from now on," said Leo.

Leo and Nick sat together talking and laughing for a while. Leo even shared his cookies. It was a very good day after all!

Leo Takes Responsibility For His Actions

By: Jack Canfield

Leo was walking home from school and he kept looking at the grade at the top of his book report. He had not done well. As he walked, he heard someone calling his name. Leo looked up to see his neighbor,

Jack, waving to him. He walked over to say hello.

"Hey Leo, why do you look so sad?" asked Jack.

"Hi Jack, I got a bad grade on my book report today," replied Leo.

"I see," said Jack. "Why do you think you didn't do well?"

"I don't think my teacher likes me very much. She didn't give me a good grade, even though I turned it in and everything," answered Leo.

"Come on over and have a seat," said Jack as he pointed toward the porch. Leo and Jack walked over to the big bench there and they both sat down.

"Did you try your very best when you were writing your report, Leo?" asked Jack.

"Well, mostly," said Leo. "It was due on Monday but I didn't want to work on it Friday night, it was the start of the weekend! I had soccer practice with my friends on Saturday and on Sunday my family watched a movie I wanted to see," said Leo.

"So when did you work on your report?"

"I flipped through the book really quick while the movie was on and then I just wrote about the things I thought were the most important," answered Leo.

"It sounds to me like your teacher gave you the grade you deserved. You can't blame her because you didn't put in a lot of effort, Leo," said Jack. "It's really important that you take responsibility for your actions. That includes the things you don't do too!"

"What do you mean?" asked Leo. "I did the report."

"Yes, but you didn't give it your full attention. Getting a bad grade was because of you. You can't blame your teacher when you didn't focus on your homework. In life, we all have to learn to take 100% responsibility for ourselves. The things that happen to us are a result of what we've done or what we didn't do."

"It's my own fault I got a bad grade, isn't it?" questioned Leo.

"I'm afraid it is buddy, however that means there is some good news," said Jack.

"What's that?"

"When you take responsibility for yourself, that means you can change! Next time you have an assignment you can make more effort and give it your best try. I bet you'll get a better grade that you can be proud of!" answered Jack.

"I can do that!" answered Leo. "In fact, I have some math problems in my bag I need to work on."

"I know you'll do your very best," said Jack as he stood up from the bench and ruffled the fur on Leo's head. Leo gave Jack a big smile and headed home. He was going to take responsibility and do great on his homework!

Say Hi To The Authors

Shaunequa Jordan - is an eagerly progressing figure within the entertainment sector. She is a best-selling author®, executive producer, director, screenwriter, and speaker. Throughout her life, she's held few authors in high regard. However, as a child she loved Maurice Sendack and Judy Blume.

Shaunequa connected to such a small pocket of writers because, in her youth, she had an odd quirk. When reading a novel, she needed to be able to SEE and visually picture, what the words were saying to her. If she could not mentally visualize the words on the page easily, she would quickly lose interest. She suffered through reading many novels over the years, but has never held this inability of fluid movement within a story against any authors. She just always chalked it up as her own personal, odd little quirk. And still does.

Besides being a goofy, quirky, individual that is a child at heart, Shaunequa is a Brooklyn, New York native (from the Bedford-Stuyvesant area). While her heart still resides in Brooklyn, her spirit is settled in Blooming Grove, New York, in the lovely Orange County of the Hudson Valley.

Craig Lack - According to *Inc.*, "Craig Lack is the most effective consultant you've never heard of." He consults with public and private C-Suites, PE Firms and independent consultants to measurably and predictably pivot OpEx into free cash flow and EBITDA.

The proprietary financial hedging strategy eliminates negligent adverse selection risk and without disrupting legacy strategy or any existing relationships.

He speaks at national conferences and to C-Suite groups. Craig has appeared in *Forbes, Inc., Fast Company, CEO Today, Huffington Post, Success, Yahoo Finance* and featured on CBS, ABC, CW and FOX.

Brittany Barocsi - is currently the Senior Editor and a Production Associate for the Dicks and Nanton Agency. There she plays an integral role in multiple projects through her content writing/editing, ghostwriting and project management skills. Prior to joining the Dicks + Nanton Agency team, Brittany enjoyed an extended internship at The Walt Disney World Resort as a cast member in the Entertainment department. Her time at Disney enticed her to move from North Carolina to Florida after graduating from Appalachian State University in May of 2012.

Brittany earned two degrees from App State, a Bachelor of Science in Communications: Public Relations and a Bachelor of Arts in English. She graduated Summa Cum Laude and earned a creative excellence award in Public Relations writing her senior year. Brittany was also a member of multiple honor societies, Lambda Pi Eta and Phi Kappa Phi, and campus organizations, including the Appalachian Popular Programming Society, Emerging Leaders Program, Dance Marathon Entertainment Chair and an Appol Corps orientation leader.

During her free time, Brittany can be found spending time with friends, traveling (especially to Caribbean destinations), running, obsessively reading her kindle, and working on writing her first novel.

 **Perminder Chohan** - is a firm believer in being genuine, honest, and trustworthy. It's these three principles that have driven him throughout his life. His efforts for authentic success has been proven, building a team of over 500 agents and focusing on helping them achieve excellence through organic, grass roots efforts in sales.

Perminder's success is notable, but it wasn't achieved without a lot of hard work. He didn't shy away from embracing opportunity, instead he began creating challenges for himself that he was determined to conquer. Perminder fed off the energy that setting goals with deadlines gave him and realized that any goal could be achieved through a solid plan, a commitment to success, and—of course—hard work!

Community involvement is another thing that Perminder is passionate about. He is a tireless supporter of many activities and events that are important to the South Asian community in the Greater Vancouver Area. His generosity and sponsorship include: fundraising for thirty-six different charities in the area, sponsoring sports activities and teams year after year, and even bringing fan favorite Bollywood acts to Canada to perform. He is also invited to present at awards ceremonies that honor various achievements.

To his community and work environment, Perminder is a valuable contributor. However, to his family he is considered a loving, caring father and husband. When asked about the factors of his success, he always expresses that none of it would be possible without the support of his loving wife, Deep, and his children, Henna and Armaan. Together, the Chohan family finds joy in being involved in their community and giving back.

Previously published books featuring Perminder are: *UnCommon* and *Performance 360 Special Edition: Success*.

Nina M. Kelly - is a mythologist (with an emphasis in depth psychology), storyteller, author, humanitarian, and cultural and arts activist. She's also an Archetypal Pattern Analyst and Dream Pattern Analyst. Nina's sense of adventure has always been sparked through learning more about people and their cultures. Believing that if you understand a person's culture, stories, myths, and rituals, then you more readily open your world to greater compassion.

Her passion for the art of healing through stories lead her to write *Grace Has A Silent Voice*, in which she honors the silent heroes and the resilience of the human spirit. Working with death and dying patients, she acquired a tremendous respect for the proper honoring of story. In *Grace Has A Silent Voice,* she acknowledges the silent heroes that walk into our lives for a moment then quickly disappear. This inevitably leaves an imprint that continues to remind us that there is beauty in humanity.

Nina is also an executive film producer for the short film *Dandelion,* as well as the former president/CEO of the Children's Bureau. There she assisted in the publication of the history of the Children's Bureau, *Saving Wednesday's Child*, authored by Mark Cave with the introduction and acknowledgements authored by Nina. Throughout her tenure, she served on numerous non-profits boards.

Furthermore, Nina is an Amazon Best-Selling Author® of three titles, *Success Breakthroughs* and *Success Mastery*, both co-authored with Jack Canfield, and *The Big Question*, coauthored with Larry King. Nina was also an Executive Producer of the first episode of the docuseries, *In Case You Didn't Know* with Nick Nanton. The premiere episode featured an indepth interview with Larry King and was entitled "Larry King: The Voice of A Generation." Additionally, Nina was an Executive Producer on the documentary, *A New Leash On Life: The K9s For Warriors Story*. The film focused on the K9s For Warriors organization, a nonprofit dedicated to helping our service men and women to overcome PTSD through the use of rescued service dogs.

Nina continues to challenge us through the inspiration and motivation of storytelling. She continues to believe that the art form of storytelling and story-sharing originate from the heart of everyone searching for expression—thus healing both listener and teller.

You may contact Nina at:
- Nina@ninastime.com
- www.ninamkelly.com

Greg Rollett - is an Emmy® Award-Winning Producer, Best-Selling Author and Marketing Expert who works with experts, authors and entrepreneurs all over the world. He utilizes the power of new media, direct response and personality-driven marketing to attract more clients and to create more freedom in the businesses and lives of his clients.

After creating a successful string of his own educational products and businesses, Greg began helping others in the production and marketing of their own products and services.

Greg has written for *Mashable, Fast Company, Inc.com, The Huffington Post, AOL, AMEX's OPEN Forum* and others, and continues to share his message helping experts and entrepreneurs grow their business through marketing. He has co-authored best-selling books with Jack Canfield, Dan Kennedy, Brian Tracy, Tom Hopkins, James Malinchak, Robert Allen, Ryan Lee and many other leading experts from around the world.

Greg's client list includes Michael Gerber, Brian Tracy, Tom Hopkins, Sally Hogshead, Coca-Cola, Miller Lite and Warner Brothers, along with thousands of entrepreneurs and small-business owners across the world. Greg's work has been featured on FOX News, ABC, NBC, CBS, CNN, *USA Today, Inc. Magazine, Fast Company, The Wall Street Journal, The Daily Buzz* and more.

To contact Greg, please visit:
* http://ambitious.com
* greg@ambitious.com

Gerri Asbury - Geraldine Asbury, M.A., CCC-SLP, is a licensed Speech Language Pathologist, nationally certified member of the American Speech Hearing Association (ASHA) and a motivational speaker. For the past 35 years as a Communication Specialist, she has dedicated her life to helping people develop their language skills to empower and support their individual needs and dreams. Currently, she presents FRESHTHINKING workshops to social groups and businesses. Gerri is fascinated with the scientific philosophies of energy and psychology and relies on both to sustain balance and harmony in her own daily life. In 2015, Gerri started integrating guided meditation paired with evidence-based Neuro-Linguistic Programming (NLP) techniques to assist clients in reframing their thoughts and releasing limiting beliefs. NLP is an extremely effective language strategy to improve memory and executive brain functions.

Gerri is a Master Wordsmith and published author. She enjoys using her WORDPOWER skills to design original acronym programs and creates daily messages that calm the mind and soothe the soul. Gerri's *GEMS* (Gerri's Expressions, Mantras & Slogans) can be used by clients of all ages to refocus their energy and uplift their moods. Daily reading of *POW* (Positive Optimistic Affirmations) can boost self-acceptance and start the day with hope and *LOVE* (Lift Our Vibrational Energy). Gerri notes that the number one benefit of teaching other people to focus their *MINDS* (Mentally Imagine New Directions & Soar) is the courage she has gained in pursuing her own dreams of writing and publishing. She believes an open mind is all that is needed to begin a new adventure and co-create your *STORY* (Start Today Openly Reassure Yourself). Say, *"YES!!"* (You Educate Society) "Life is *WILD*" (World Invites Living Dreams).

As a Celebrity Expert® in self-confidence, Gerri shares the key to connecting with your inner *STAR* (Strengths, Talents, Abilities, & Resources). Her current mission is to expand her services to incorporate online technology to help more people *THRIVE* (Trust Heart, Reconnect, Ignite Vibrant Expression) with a 30-day challenge called "The *ASBURY* Program: Achieve Success Breakthroughs & Unleash Radiant You." Each one of us is on a sacred mission to find and build our *SELF-CONFIDENCE* (Spirit's Eternal Life Force-Claim Ownership, Nurture Feelings, Identity, Dreams, Emotions, Never-ending Compassion & Exuberance). Gerri believes in the sacred birthright of *JOY* (Journey Of You). According to Dale Carnegie, "The sweetest sound in any language is the sound of your name." Consequently, parents lovingly choose the perfect name for each newborn. All words carry unique vibrational frequencies and personal names can fuel loving bonds and nurturing energy. Self-Confidence and knowing who we are can be empowering strengths when life feels hard. Remember to turn inward and rely on your *GIFTS* (Great Imagination, Fabulous Talents, & Skills) to reclaim your *JOY!*

Connect with Geraldine Asbury to rediscover your *STAR* qualities at:
- Asburywordpower@gmail.com

Edward Mafoud - Edward Mafoud is the head of one of the most creative and exciting bakeries in the world, Damascus Bakeries. There the culture centers around pleasing fans with the Flat Bread Experience: Artisanal Flavor and Texture embodied in a Flat Bread. Edward loves watching their Warriors (employees) at work in their facilities. They know that they are part of something special and exhibit all the craft and enthusiasm of artisans at work.

Edward has served as a Producer on multiple films directed by Nick Nanton, including *Rudy Ruettiger: The Walk On, Getting Everything You Can Out of All You've Got: The Jay Abraham Story*, as well as the upcoming *Folds of Honor* film.

Sheri Hays - began working with children at an early age. In college, she worked at a day care center during the school year and children's camps during the summer. This led her to pursue her Bachelor of Science degree in Early Childhood Education at Berry College. Afterwards, she enjoyed teaching Kindergarten for five years.

In 2000, with a daughter on the way and her husband's law firm expanding, Sheri decided to focus on raising her own child and working as the Assistant Director of Community Outreach at the Law offices of Gary Martin Hays and Associates. There she helped to raise money and awareness for charities including Relay for Life, St. Jude Children's Research Hospital, Dream House for Medically Fragile Children, and Families 4 Families. To date they have given away 1000 bicycle helmets and 16 college scholarships.

In 2006, after the birth of her twin daughters, she helped her husband begin the non-profit organization, Keep Georgia Safe. The organization's mission is to provide safety education and crime prevention training in Georgia. Keep Georgia Safe has trained over 80 state and local law enforcement officers in CART (Child Abduction Response Teams) to ensure first responders know what to do in the event a child is abducted. It has also provided training and instructor certification for dozens of officers, teachers, and volunteers in the radKids curriculum. After their certification, these instructors have taught this safety curriculum to hundreds of children.

Today, Sheri continues to raise her three beautiful daughters and to serve her community. In her spare time, she enjoys teaching children at church, volunteering in the elementary school library, and writing children's books. Sheri, Gary, and their three daughters reside in Atlanta, Georgia.

 **Rosie Unite** - is Founder and CEO of ImaginateLife®, a for-profit global social impact venture that was born from an unexpected, extraordinary event that forever transformed her life.

She is passionate about the power of neuroscience, epigenetics, quantum physics, and spirituality to heal bodies, elevate minds, and transform lives. Known as The Possibilities Whisperer®, Rosie shares her own extraordinary transformation to help others through keynote speeches, workshops, and advisory services.

She is grateful for her greatest teacher-of-life, Dr. Joe Dispenza, the compassionate visionary, neuroscientist, educator, and *New York Times* best-selling author. She is honored to have participated in his global research on meditation effects on the brain and body. She has been QEEG brain-mapped by neuroscientists and measured for heart coherence by HeartMath Institute.

Rosie is a lifelong student of holistic learning, leading and service.

- Wharton MBA
- ThoughtLeader® Summit Participant
- National Association of Experts, Writers & Speakers® Member
- National Academy of Best-Selling Authors® Member

- Recipient of three Quilly® Awards: Co-authored books *The Big Question* (Larry King); *Professional Performance 360 Special Edition: Success, 2nd Edition* (Richard Branson); *Success Breakthroughs* (Jack Canfield)
- Certified Trainer: *The Success Principles™, Canfield Methodology™*
- Recipient of two EXPY® Awards: Co-authored children's book *Leo Learns About Life*, Executive Producer of documentary film *The Voice of a Generation: An Evening with Larry King*
- Featured on: ABC, NBC, CBS, Fox, *Success Today®, USA Today, Wall Street Journal*
- Keynotes: *Success LIVE™, Women Economic Forum* ("Iconic Women, Better World" Award), *Global Entrepreneurship Initiative®* hosted at United Nations Headquarters

In her 30-year global career, Rosie has been a leader in social impact and Fortune 500 corporates.

- Helped build, launch and grow new companies and mobile, telecommunications, and digital technologies
- Worked with Sprint, GTE/Verizon, DoubleClick/Google, Johnson & Johnson, Silicon Graphics/HP Enterprise, France Telecom, Deutsche Telekom, IDB, World Bank, Academy for Educational Development, Habitat for Humanity, and Peace Corps

A Sivananda Hatha Yoga Certified Instructor, Rosie has also:

- Completed: Vipassana 10-Day Meditation, EFT Universe Certification Program Levels 1-2-3 (Tapping).
- Fulfilled a childhood dream by traveling in 65 countries and living in eight: USA, Brazil, Netherlands, Hong Kong, Spain, Bulgaria, Dominican Republic, and UK.

Lindsay Dicks - helps her clients tell their stories in the online world. Being brought up around a family of marketers, but a product of Generation Y, Lindsay naturally gravitated to the new world of on-line marketing. Lindsay began freelance writing in 2000 and soon after launched her own PR firm that thrived by offering an in-your-face "Guaranteed PR" that was one of the first of its type in the nation.

Lindsay's new media career is centered on her philosophy that "people buy people." Her goal is to help her clients build a relationship with their prospects and customers. Once that relationship is built and they learn to trust them as the expert in their field, then they will do business with them. Lindsay also built a proprietary process that utilizes social media marketing, content marketing and search engine optimization to create online "buzz" for her clients that helps them to convey their business and personal story. Lindsay's clientele spans the entire business map and ranges from doctors and small business owners to Inc. 500 CEOs.

Lindsay is a graduate of the University of Florida. She is the CEO of CelebritySites™, an online marketing company specializing in social media and online personal branding. Lindsay is recognized as one of the top online marketing experts in the world and has co-authored more than 25 best-selling books alongside authors such as Steve Forbes, Richard Branson, Brian Tracy, Jack Canfield (creator of the *Chicken Soup for the Soul* series), Dan Kennedy, Robert Allen, Dr. Ivan Misner (founder of BNI), Jay Conrad Levinson (author of the *Guerilla Marketing* series), Leigh Steinberg and many others, including the breakthrough hit, *Celebrity Branding You!*

She has also been selected as one of America's PremierExperts™ and has been quoted in *Forbes, Newsweek, The Wall Street Journal, USA Today,* and *Inc. Magazine* as well as featured on NBC, ABC, and CBS television affiliates speaking on social media, search engine optimization and making more money online. Lindsay was also recently brought on FOX 35 News as their Online Marketing Expert.

Lindsay, a national speaker, has shared the stage with some of the top speakers in the world, including Brian Tracy, Lee Milteer, Ron LeGrand, Arielle Ford, Leigh Steinberg, Dr. Nido Qubein, Dan Sullivan, David Bullock, Peter Shankman and many others. Lindsay was also a Producer on the Emmy®-winning film, *Jacob's Turn*, and sits on the advisory board for the Global Economic Initiative.

You can connect with Lindsay at:
- Lindsay@CelebritySites.com
- www.twitter.com/LindsayMDicks
- www.facebook.com/LindsayDicks

 **Dr. Darren Tong** - For over 28 years, Dr. Darren Tong has been one of the most trusted pediatric dentists in Bergen and Rockland Counties. Dr. Tong earned his doctor of dental medicine from Columbia University College of Dental Medicine, graduating in the top 10% of his class. He then completed his advanced specialty training in Pediatric Dentistry at the prestigious Schneider's Children's Hospital in Long Island, NY.

Dr. Tong's vision of his pediatric dental office, Smile More Kidz, has materialized into an exceptional dental experience for his pediatric patients. The children feel comfortable, well taken care of, and safe. His dental office has received the "Talk of the Town" award in patient satisfaction.

Dr. Tong has co-authored a best-selling book, *Dare to Succeed,* alongside Jack Canfield. He has also appeared on the *America's Premier Experts* TV show to share his knowledge on dentistry, which aired on ABC, NBC, CBS, Fox and their affiliates. Dr. Tong is also an executive producer of the forthcoming documentary about the Folds of Honor organization. Folds of Honor is a non-profit company that provides educational scholarships to spouses and children of America's fallen and disabled service members.

Dr. Tong is married with five children, ranging from ages 25 to 12, so he is very familiar with the struggles and rewards parents experience in raising children. When you see Dr. Tong interact with your children, you'll know right away why he was voted Favorite Kid's Doc in NJ's parent magazine many times over.

To learn more about Dr. Tong and his office, please visit: www.SmileMoreKidz.com or visit one of their two locations:

Washington Dental Associates
19 Legion Drive
Bergenfield, NJ 07675
201-384-2425

or

Smile More Dentistry /
Smile More Kidz
140 Oak Tree Road
Tappan, NY 10983
845-359-1763

 **Dean Collins** - Dean (DAC) Collins has built a brand around inspiring music instruction. His love for music developed into a passion for learning and teaching others to play the guitar and harmonica together…it's easy for kids to learn and equally effective and simple for adults. Adults can take their "I've always wanted to play" dreams and begin playing their favorite songs using an easy 1-2-3 method.

DAC has reinvented himself with a new part-time career focused on powerful messaging and music instruction, product development and becoming a Best-Selling Author®. DAC has translated powerful time-tested success principles to kids in subtle messaging while teaching their favorite songs via guitar and harmonica instruction. DAC has patent pending products including "The Harmonica Holder," which makes it easier for kids and adults to play the guitar and harmonica simultaneously. He is currently seeking licensing agreements with interested companies.

DAC is a graduate of the University of Alabama at Birmingham with a degree in Criminal Justice. He is currently a full time LEO (Law Enforcement Officer) and a multiple award-winning member of the Ohio Air Force National Guard. He has nearly 20 years experience in both fields.

In his spare time, DAC relaxes by running his non-profit, organization—flagpolesforvets.org—and playing in his band at various venues, including anywhere veterans and music lovers gather. The D. DAC Collins Band is a local favorite playing a mix of Country, 70's/80's rock and gospel.

You can connect with DAC at:
  • www.facebook.com/DACCollinsHarpArm

JW Dicks, Esq. - is a Business Development Attorney, a *Wall Street Journal* Best-Selling Author®—who has authored over 47 books—and a 5x Emmy® Award-winning Executive Producer and a Broadway Show Producer.

JW is an XPrize Innovation Board member, Chairman of the Board of the National Academy of Best-Selling Authors®, Board Member of the National Association of Experts, Writers and Speakers®, Board Member of the International Academy of Film Makers® and Board Member of the National Retirement Council™.

JW is the CEO of DNAgency, an Inc. 5000 Multi Media Company that represents over 3,694 clients in 65 countries. He has been quoted on business and financial topics in national media such as *USA Today, The Wall Street Journal, Newsweek, Forbes*, CNBC.com, and *Fortune Magazine Small Business.*

Considered a Thoughtleader® and curator of information, JW has co-authored books with legends like Jack Canfield, Brian Tracy, Tom Hopkins, Dr. Nido Qubein, Steve Forbes, Richard Branson, Michael Gerber, Dr. Ivan Misner, and Dan Kennedy.

JW has appeared on business television shows airing on ABC, NBC, CBS, and FOX affiliates around the country and coproduces and syndicates a line of franchised business television shows such as *Success Today®, Wall Street Today®, Hollywood Live*™, and *Profiles of Success®.*

JW and his wife of 47 years, Linda, have two daughters and four granddaughters. He is a sixth-generation Floridian and splits his time between his home in Orlando and his beach house on Florida's west coast.

Dr. Carmella Montez Knoernschild - One of the first female Orthodontists in Arkansas, Dr. Carmella Montez Knoernschild (Dr. K) earned her Certificate of Advanced Graduate Study in Orthodontics in 1990 from Boston University. There she was inducted into the university's honorary dental society, Omicron Kappa Upsilon, and has continued to excel in the field of Orthodontics ever since.

Currently, Dr. K is the President, Owner, and primary Orthodontist at Carmella Montez Knoernschild, DDS, PA. Some of her professional accolades include: Becoming a certified Diplomate of the American Board of Orthodontics in 2003, serving as the technical advisor for the Arkansas Association of Orthodontist's video, "A Smile That's Good for Life," and receiving the Arkansas State Dental Association's "New Dentist of the Year" award. Dr. K is also an active member of many professional and community associations such as: President, Arkansas Association of Orthodontists; The Southwestern Society of Orthodontists; The American Association of Orthodontists; The University of Arkansas Alumni Association; and The Russellville Area Chamber of Commerce. Along with the many professional associations she participates in, Dr. K is enthusiastic about motivating young people. She sponsors various local youth sporting events and serves as a motivational speaker.

Dr. Knoernschild and her husband, Doug, along with their beautiful girls, Ciarra and Isabella, reside near Lamar and attend New Life Church in Russellville, Arkansas.

 **Nick Nanton** - An Emmy® Award-Winning Director and Producer, Nick Nanton, Esq., produces media and branded content for top thought leaders and media personalities around the world. Recognized as a leading expert on branding and storytelling, Nick has authored more than two dozen Best-Selling books (including *The Wall Street Journal* Best-Seller, *StorySelling*™) and produced and directed more than 50 documentaries, earning 11 Emmy® wins and 25 nominations. Nick speaks to audiences internationally on the topics of branding, entertainment, media, business and storytelling at major universities and events.

As the CEO of DNA Media, Nick oversees a portfolio of companies including: The Dicks + Nanton Agency (an international agency with more than 3,694 clients in 65 countries), Dicks + Nanton Productions, Ambitious.com and DNA Films. Nick is an award-winning director, producer and songwriter who has worked on everything from large scale events to television shows with the likes of Steve Forbes, Ivanka Trump, Sir Richard Branson, Rudy Ruettiger (inspiration for the Hollywood Blockbuster, *Rudy*), Brian Tracy, Jack Canfield (*The Secret*, creator of the *Chicken Soup for the Soul* Series), Michael E. Gerber, Tom Hopkins, Dan Kennedy and many more.

Nick has been seen in *USA Today, The Wall Street Journal, Newsweek, BusinessWeek, Inc. Magazine, The New York Times, Entrepreneur® Magazine, Forbes, FastCompany*, and has appeared on ABC, NBC, CBS, and FOX television affiliates across the country as well as on CNN, FOX News, CNBC, and MSNBC from coast to coast.

Nick is a member of the Florida Bar, a member of The National Academy of Television Arts & Sciences (Home to the EMMYs®), Co-founder of The National Academy of Best-Selling Authors®, and serves on the Innovation Board of the XPRIZE Foundation, a non-profit organization dedicated to bringing about "radical breakthroughs for the benefit of humanity" through incentivized competition, best known for its Ansari XPRIZE which incentivized the first private space flight and was the catalyst for Richard Branson's Virgin Galactic.

Nick also enjoys serving as an Elder at Orangewood Church, working with Young Life, Downtown Credo Orlando, Entrepreneurs International and rooting for the Florida Gators with his wife Kristina and their three children, Brock, Bowen and Addison.
Learn more at:
  • www.NickNanton.com
  • www.CelebrityBrandingAgency.com

 **Jack Canfield** - Known as America's #1 Success Coach, Jack Canfield is the CEO of the Canfield Training Group in Santa Barbara, CA, which trains and coaches entrepreneurs, corporate leaders, managers, sales professionals and the general public in how to accelerate the achievement of their personal, professional and financial goals.

Jack Canfield is best known as the coauthor of the #1 *New York Times* bestselling *Chicken Soup for the Soul®* book series, which has sold more than 500 million books in 47 languages, including 11 *New York Times* #1 bestsellers. As the CEO of Chicken Soup for the Soul Enterprises he helped grow the *Chicken Soup for the Soul®* brand into a virtual empire of books, children's books, audios, videos, CDs, classroom materials, a syndicated column and a television show, as well as a vigorous program of licensed products that includes everything from clothing and board games to nutraceuticals and a successful line of *Chicken Soup for the Pet Lover's Soul®* cat and dog foods.

His other books include *The Success Principles™: How to Get from Where You Are to Where You Want to Be* (recently revised as the 10th Anniversary Edition), *The Success Principles for Teens, The Aladdin Factor, Dare to Win, Heart at Work, The Power of Focus: How to Hit Your Personal, Financial and Business Goals with Absolute Certainty, You've Got to Read This Book, Tapping into Ultimate Success, Jack Canfield's Key to Living the Law of Attraction,* his recent novel, *The Golden Motorcycle Gang: A Story of Transformation and The 30-Day Sobriety Solution.*

Jack is a dynamic speaker and was recently inducted into the National Speakers Association's Speakers Hall of Fame. He has appeared on more than 1000 radio and television shows including Oprah, Montel, Larry King Live, the Today Show, Fox and Friends, and 2 hour-long PBS Specials devoted exclusively to his work. Jack is also a featured teacher in 12 movies including *The Secret, The Meta-Secret, The Truth, The Keeper of the Keys, Tapping into the Source,* and *The Tapping Solution.* Jack was also honored recently with a documentary that was produced about his life and teachings, *The Soul of Success: The Jack Canfield Story.*

Jack has personally helped hundreds of thousands of people on six different continents become multi-millionaires, business leaders, best-selling authors, leading sales professionals, successful entrepreneurs, and world-class athletes while at the same time creating balanced, fulfilling and healthy lives.

His corporate clients have included Virgin Records, SONY Pictures, Daimler-Chrysler, Federal Express, GE, Johnson & Johnson, Merrill Lynch, Campbell's Soup, Re/Max, The Million Dollar Forum, The Million Dollar Roundtable, The Young Entrepreneurs Organization, The Young Presidents Organization, the Executive Committee, and the World Business Council.

Jack is the founder of the Transformational Leadership Council and a member of Evolutionary Leaders, two groups devoted to helping create a world that works for everyone.

Jack is a graduate of Harvard, earned his M.Ed. from the University of Massachusetts, and has received three honorary doctorates in psychology and public service. He is married, has three children, two step-children and a grandson.

For more information, visit:
- www.JackCanfield.com
- www.CanfieldTraintheTrainer.com

CPSIA information can be obtained
at www.ICGtesting.com
Printed in the USA
BVHW050458180619
551232BV00002B/5/P